David Copperfield

Artists: Penko Gelev
Sotir Gelev

First edition for North America (including Canada and Mexico),
Philippine Islands, and Puerto Rico published in 2011
by Barron's Educational Series, Inc.

All inquiries should be addressed to:
Barron's Educational Series, Inc.
250 Wireless Boulevard
Hauppauge, NY 11788
www.barronseduc.com

ISBN (Hardcover): 978-0-7641-6305-0
ISBN (Paperback): 978-0-7641-4453-0

Library of Congress Control No.: 2010939397

Picture credits:
p. 40 © Coll. Jaime Abecasis/Topfoto.co.uk
p. 43 (L) David Antram, (R) Carolyn Franklin

Every effort has been made to trace copyright holders. The Salariya Book Company apologizes for
any omissions and would be pleased, in such cases, to add an acknowledgment in future editions.

Date of Manufacture: July 2011
Manufactured by: Leo Paper Products, Ltd., Heshan, Guangdong, China
Printed and bound in China.
Printed on paper from sustainable sources.
9 8 7 6 5 4 3 2 1

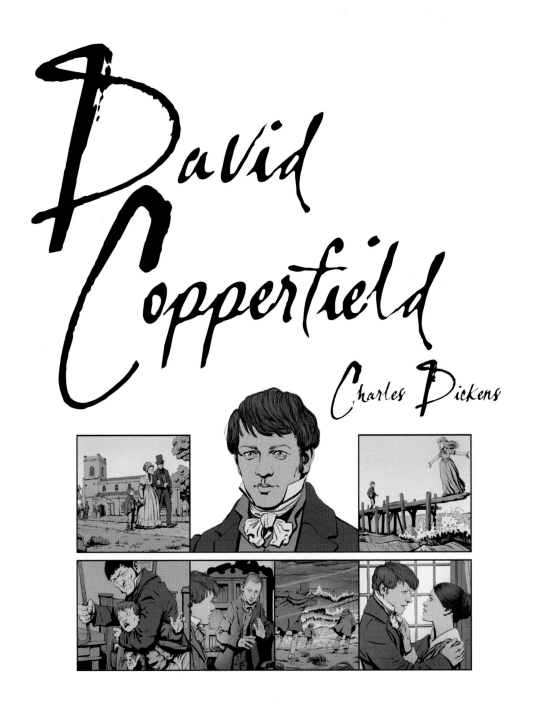

David Copperfield

Charles Dickens

Illustrated by

Penko Gelev

Retold by

Jacqueline Morley

Series created and designed by

David Salariya

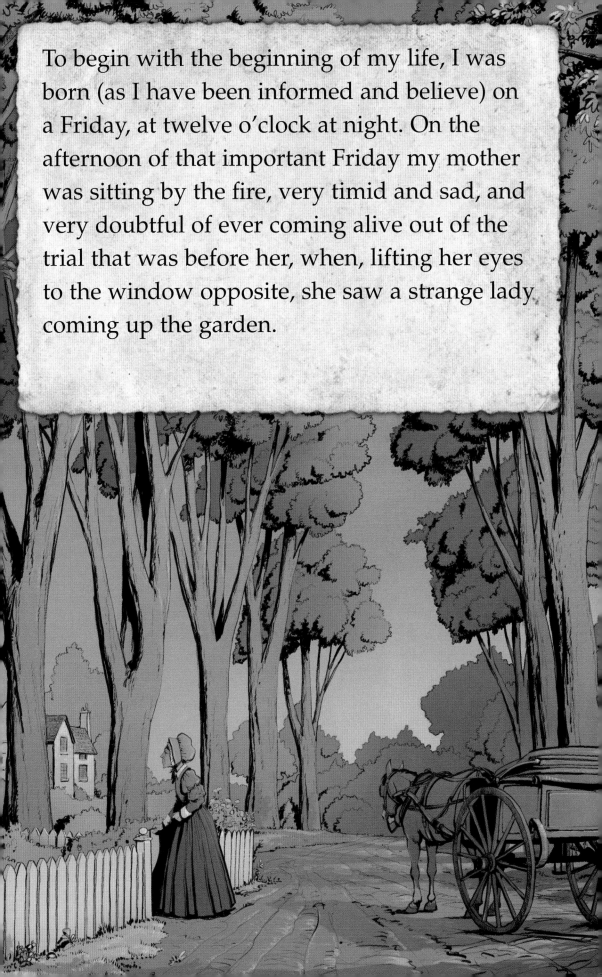

To begin with the beginning of my life, I was born (as I have been informed and believe) on a Friday, at twelve o'clock at night. On the afternoon of that important Friday my mother was sitting by the fire, very timid and sad, and very doubtful of ever coming alive out of the trial that was before her, when, lifting her eyes to the window opposite, she saw a strange lady coming up the garden.

CHARACTERS

David Copperfield

Clara Peggotty,
David's nurse

Miss Betsey Trotwood,
David's great-aunt

Mr. Edward Murdstone,
David's stepfather

Miss Jane Murdstone,
Mr. Murdstone's sister

Mr. Daniel Peggotty,
Clara Peggotty's brother

Ham, Mr. Peggotty's
orphaned nephew

Emily, Mr. Peggotty's
orphaned niece

James Steerforth

Thomas Traddles

Mr. Wickfield,
a lawyer

Agnes,
his daughter

Uriah Heep,
Mr. Wickfield's clerk

Mr. Dick, a relative of
Miss Trotwood

Mr. Wilkins
Micawber

Dora Spenlow

I Am Born

My mother, recently widowed, was by the fire, feeling rather unwell, when she saw a face looking in at the window.

It was her husband's aunt, Miss Betsey Trotwood, an alarming and most eccentric person she had heard about but never met.

You need some tea. I'll call your maid. What is her name?

Peggotty.

Peggotty! Do you mean that any human being has got herself christened Peggotty?

It's her surname.

My husband called her by it because her Christian name is the same as mine.

Here! Peggotty! Your mistress is unwell. Don't dawdle.

Now, child, from the moment of the birth of this girl...

Perhaps boy.

Don't contradict. I intend to be her godmother, and I beg you'll call her Betsey Trotwood Copperfield.

Peggotty sent for the doctor. My great-aunt did not budge until the doctor brought her the good news.

Well, ma'am, I am happy to congratulate you. All is now over, and well over.

How is she?

Quite as comfortable as we can expect a young mother to be.

And *she*? The baby. How is she?

Ma'am, I apprehended[1] you had known. It's a boy.

My aunt aimed a blow at the doctor's head with her bonnet, put it on bent, walked out, and never came back.

1. apprehended: thought.

7

TWO SURPRISES

I grew up very happily with Mama and Peggotty. I was still small, just old enough to read, when a gentleman with black whiskers began walking back from church with us.

Peggotty seemed uneasy about this gentleman. I did not like him at all.

Not such a one as this Mr. Copperfield[1] wouldn't have liked. That I say and that I swear.

If people are so silly as to seem to admire me, is it my fault?

One day Peggotty made an unusual suggestion.

Would you like to stay with me at my brother's at Yarmouth[2] for a fortnight? He's a fisherman.

I would indeed.

We went to Yarmouth in the carrier's[3] cart. Peggotty's nephew, Ham, carried me on his shoulders down to a strange house on the sea shore.

Yon's[4] our house, Mas'r Davy.

That ship-looking thing?

Glad to see you, Sir. We shall be proud of your company.

The old boat was the most wonderful house in the world, so neat and tidy inside. Mr. Peggotty gave us a rousing welcome.

Mr. Peggotty had adopted Ham and Emily. They were cousins, the orphaned children of his brother and sister.

He is as good as gold and as true as steel.

He had even given a home to depressed Mrs. Gummidge, the widow of his business partner.

1. Mr. Copperfield: David's late father, who was also called David Copperfield.
2. Yarmouth: Great Yarmouth in Norfolk, a seaside resort which at this time was famous for herring fishing. For places mentioned in the story, see the map on page 43.
3. carrier: the local delivery man.   4. Yon: Over there. Ham speaks a rustic Norfolk dialect.

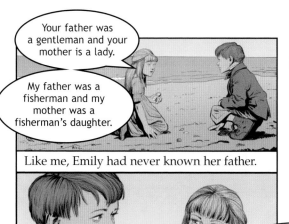

Your father was a gentleman and your mother is a lady.

My father was a fisherman and my mother was a fisherman's daughter.

Like me, Emily had never known her father.

I'm not afraid of the sea — but it's cruel to some of our men.

Would you like to be a lady?

Very much! I'd give Uncle Dan a coat with diamond buttons and a box of money.

I was in love with Emily!

But the days sped by and soon we were home again. I ran indoors to fling my arms around Mama. She was not there.

Why, Peggotty! Isn't she come home?

Yes, yes, Mas'r Davy. Wait a bit and I'll — I'll tell you something.

I should have told you before but I couldn't azackly[1] bring my mind to it.

What do you think? You have got a Pa — a new one!

I don't want to see him.

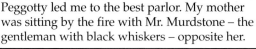

Now, Clara my dear. Recollect! Control yourself, always control yourself.

Davy, boy, how do you do?

Peggotty led me to the best parlor. My mother was sitting by the fire with Mr. Murdstone – the gentleman with black whiskers – opposite her.

My mother kissed me nervously and went on with her work. No one seemed to want me. I went to bed and cried myself to sleep.

1. azackly: Peggotty's way of saying "exactly."

I Am Wicked

David, if I have an obstinate[1] horse or dog to deal with, what do I do?

I don't know.

Mr. Murdstone was not pleased.

I beat him. I say to myself, "I'll conquer that fellow." Wash your face, Sir, and come down.

If I had not obeyed, he would have knocked me down.

Generally speaking, I don't like boys. How d'ye do, boy?

Very well, ma'am, I — I —

Wants manners!

Mr. Murdstone's sister, a very grim lady, came to live with us, to "help" my mother.

If I go into a cheese shop and buy 5,000 double Gloucester cheeses at 4½ pence each, what do I pay?[2]

Timid Mama was easily persuaded that her husband knew best. Lessons became a torment.

Now, David, you must be far more careful today than usual.

I was used to Mr. Murdstone throwing a book at me, but one day he had a cane in his hands.

Mr. Murdstone, Sir, pray don't beat me. I can't learn when you and Miss Murdstone are by.

The lesson started badly and went on worse. Mr. Murdstone marched me to my room and twisted my head under his arm.

AAARRGH!

I seized the hand that held me and bit it through.

10   1. obstinate: stubborn.
      2. what do I pay?: Until 1971, there were 12 pence in a shilling and 20 shillings in a pound, so the question was much more complicated than it would seem to be (answer on page 45).

He beat me as if he would have beaten me to death.

I was locked in my room for five days. Miss Murdstone let me out for half an hour each day and I saw no one else.

To cure my wickedness I was to be sent to school in London.

For you, my poppet,[1] from me and your mama.

I was on my way to pick up the London coach when Peggotty burst from a hedge and thrust a purse and a bag of cakes at me.

When she was gone I offered Mr. Barkis, the carrier, a cake. He was a very silent man, but the cake prompted a remark.

Did *she* make 'em, now?

Ah! Her.

Yes. She does all our cooking.

Peggotty, do you mean, Sir?

No sweethearts, I b'lieve?

Oh, no. She never had a sweetheart.

P'raps you might be writin' to her? If you was, p'raps you'd recollect to say that Barkis was willin'.[2]

He could easily speak to Peggotty himself, I thought, but I sent a letter from Yarmouth while waiting for the coach to London.

I was met in London by a master from my new school, Salem House – a dismal place. In the schoolroom he tied a placard[3] on my back.

TAKE CARE. HE BITES.

1. my poppet: my dear.   2. Barkis was willin': Barkis would be willing to be Peggotty's sweetheart.
3. placard: sign.

AT SCHOOL

I was taken to meet Mr. Creakle, the headmaster.

I have the happiness of knowing your stepfather.[1] He knows me, and I know him. Do *you* know me? Hey?

Not yet, Sir.

You will soon. I'll tell you what I am. I'm a Tartar.[2]

I dreaded being tormented over the placard, but a kind boy called Tommy Traddles made a good-natured joke of it.

Look here! Here's a game!

The most important boy in the school was James Steerforth. He was clever and handsome, and at least 16.

What money have you got?

Seven shillings.

You had better let me take care of it.

It was such a friendly suggestion that I emptied Peggotty's purse into his hand.

Perhaps you'd like to spend a couple of shillings on currant wine?

Another shilling or so on almond cakes? We must stretch it as far as we can.

There you are, young Copperfield, and a royal spread you've got.

I feared this was a waste of my mother's money. But I forgot this in the glory of the feast that night. Steerforth promised to look after me. How I admired him, as I looked at him asleep in the moonlight, his handsome head resting easily on his arm.

1. stepfather: Dickens actually uses the word "father-in-law," which has an entirely different meaning in modern English.
2. Tartar: a person who insists on strict discipline.

The ignorant Mr. Creakle ruled by terror.

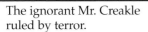

He did away with my placard because it got in the way of his cane.

One day I had surprise visitors: Mr. Peggotty and Ham.

Mr. Steerforth is very kind to me.

You should see their house, Steerforth. It's made out of a boat.

The right sort of house for such a thorough-built boatman.

It's at your service if ever you should come along with Mas'r Davy.

Steerforth's charming, friendly manner put them at their ease at once.

On the way home for the holidays I told Mr. Barkis I had sent his message. He thought hard and gave me another.

Says you, "Peggotty! Barkis is waitin' for a answer."

Says she, perhaps, "Answer to what?"

Says you, "To what I told you."

"What is that?" says she.

"Barkis is willin'," says you.

Davy, my pretty boy! This is your brother.

When I got home I could hear my mother singing softly in the old parlor. I looked in.

Peggotty, dear, you are not going to marry Barkis?

Don't leave me, Peggotty. It will not be for long, perhaps.

Me leave you? What's put that in your silly little head?

Miss Murdstone could not wait to see the back of me. She checked off each day of my vacation on the calendar.

The Murdstones would not be home till late. Peggotty, Mama, and I spent the happiest evening around the fire, though Mama looked pale and tired.

I will never forget my mother's sad figure waving good-bye.

I Am Rejected

On my birthday I was called to Mr. Creakle's office. I found Mrs. Creakle there, with a strange look on her face.

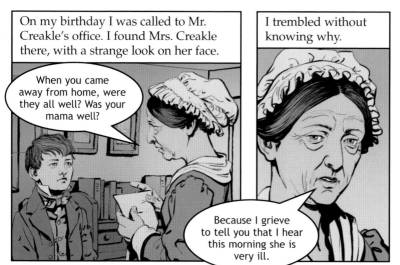

> When you came away from home, were they all well? Was your mama well?

> Because I grieve to tell you that I hear this morning she is very ill.

I trembled without knowing why.

> She is dead.

There was no need to say it. I knew before she had spoken, and gave a desolate cry.

I went home the next day for a double funeral. My little brother had not outlasted his mother a day.

Peggotty asked to take me to her brother's for a couple of weeks.

> Humph! He will be idle there, and idleness is the root of all evil. But he would be idle anywhere, so I had better say yes.

Mr. Barkis had as little to say as usual, but gave Peggotty so many nudges that I got completely squashed.

> Are you pretty comfortable? Are you? Really and truly pretty comfortable? Are you? Eh?

> A little puss, it is!

> So sh'is! So sh'is, Mas'r Davy bor',[1] so sh'is.

The boat-house seemed smaller now, and Emily was much more grown-up. She teased me and would not play. Everyone spoiled her.

1. bor': a friendly form of address, probably short for "neighbor."

And how's your friend, Sir?

Steerforth?

That's the name. There's a friend, if you talk of friends! Lord love my heart alive, if it ain't a treat to look at him!

He is very handsome, is he not? And astonishingly clever. He's as brave as a lion and such a generous noble fellow. It's hardly possible to praise him enough.

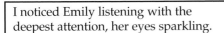
I noticed Emily listening with the deepest attention, her eyes sparkling.

Em'ly is like me, and would like to see him.

One day Barkis took Emily and me and Peggotty for an outing. The others gave us a special send-off – apparently we were on our way to Peggotty and Barkis's wedding!

It'll go contrary with me. Things always do. You had better do it yourself.

You do it, Mrs. Gummidge!

Come on, old gal. Heave the shoe at them.[1]

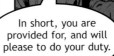

I returned home to total neglect, not sent back to school and not taught at home. One day, Mr. Murdstone had a visitor.

David, education is costly.

What is before you is a fight with the world; and the sooner you begin it, the better.

Mr. Quinion is my manager at Murdstone and Grinby.

In his employment you will earn enough for food and pocket money. Your lodging will be paid by me.

In short, you are provided for, and will please to do your duty.

I quite understood that they were getting rid of me. And so at the age of 10 I was sent to London as a boy laborer.

1. Heave the shoe at them: It was tradition to throw an old shoe after the bride and groom to wish them luck.

ON MY OWN

At Murdstone and Grinby's bottling factory, I washed bottles or pasted labels all day.

> My dear Master Copperfield. I hope I see you well, Sir.

I was introduced to my landlord, Mr. Micawber. He was a salesman for the firm, but made very few sales.

Mr. Micawber had a rather grand way of speaking, but he was kindness itself.

Mrs. Micawber was nursing twins, and had two other children besides.

The Micawbers could never pay their bills, but lived in hopes of something "turning up."

> Blood cannot be obtained from a stone.

Mrs. Micawber often sent me to the pawn shop[1] to raise money on cutlery and household things.

> No man is without a friend who is possessed of shaving materials.[2]

At one moment, Mr. Micawber claimed to be considering suicide…

> A hot kidney pudding and a plate of shrimps.

… and the next minute he was gleefully ordering tomorrow's breakfast.

Finally he was taken away to a debtors' prison.

> Remember: income twenty pounds, expenditure nineteen pounds, nineteen shillings and sixpence — result, happiness.

> Expenditure twenty pounds and sixpence — result, misery.

1. pawn shop: a shop where money can be borrowed by leaving valuable goods in exchange.
2. shaving materials: Before safety blades were invented, men shaved with folding knives called "cut-throat" razors. Mr. Micawber threatens to kill himself with one of these.

Arrangements with Mr. Micawber's creditors[1] resulted in his release. He now hoped to find work in the Customs House in Plymouth.[2]

In case something turns up?

Exactly!

We think he must be on the spot.

Master Copperfield, God bless you!

When I went to see them off on the stagecoach, Mrs. Micawber gave me a great hug. I think she realized for the first time how young I was. Without the Micawbers, life would be grim.

I decided to run away to the only relative I had – my aunt, Miss Trotwood. I hired a man with a cart – that was a mistake.

Stop! He's got my box and my money!

Panting and crying, but never thinking of giving up, I started on the road to Dover with only three halfpence in my pocket.

What do you want for this little weskit?[3]

Would eighteen pence be...

I should rob my family if I was to offer ninepence.

Remembering my errands for Mrs. Micawber, I took off my waistcoat and went into a shop marked GENTS' WARDROBES BOUGHT.

I slept rough that night, and had to pawn my jacket too. Two days later, blistered, tattered, and starving, I reached my aunt's cottage.

If you please, Aunt...

Go away! Go along! No boys here!

My aunt was so surprised, she sat down flat on the garden path.

Eh?

If you please, Aunt, I am your nephew.

Oh, Lord!

1. creditors: the people to whom he owed money.
2. Plymouth: a seaport in the southwest of England.
3. weskit: waistcoat or vest.

I Find a New Life

My aunt marched me into the parlor and stretched me out on the sofa. She asked her maid to fetch Mr. Dick.

Mr. Dick, here is my nephew, David Copperfield. What shall I do with him?

I should wash him.

There, Janet, Mr. Dick sets us all to rights. Heat the bath!

At first Mr. Dick stared so vacantly at me that I thought he was not quite right in the head – but I saw that my aunt trusted and relied on him.

While Janet was getting the bath ready, my aunt suddenly stiffened with rage.

Janet! Donkeys!

My aunt waged a constant battle to stop people riding donkeys over the little green in front of her cottage.

Mr. Dick's family had put him in an asylum,[1] but my aunt had taken him to live with her. He was trying to write a history of his life.

When Charles I[2] was executed, they took the trouble out of his head and put it in mine.

My aunt had written to the Murdstones, and they were coming to discuss me.

Go along with you! You have no business here. Go along, you bold-faced thing.

Miss Murdstone hired a donkey to get up the hill, and got the full force of my aunt's rage. It was not a good beginning.

I'll take my chance with the boy, if he is as you say he is. But I don't believe a word of it.

My aunt listened, stony-faced, to Mr. Murdstone's account of my bad character. Then she sent them away.

1. asylum: an early form of mental hospital.
2. Charles I: king of England and Scotland, 1625–1649. He was executed by the Parliamentarians at the end of the English Civil War.

Despite her fierce manner, my aunt was very fond of me. She decided to call me Trotwood Copperfield, after herself.

Very much.

Trot, we must not forget your education. Should you like to go to school in Canterbury?[1]

So I began a new life, with a new name.

Is Mr. Wickfield at home, Uriah Heep?

Mr. Wickfield's at home, ma'am, if you'll please to walk in.

Next day we drove to Canterbury to ask Mr. Wickfield, my aunt's lawyer, for his advice about schools. A long, lank, sunken-faced youth came to the door.

This is my little housekeeper, Agnes.

Mr. Wickfield recommended Dr. Strong's school. I would live with Mr. Wickfield. He was a widower, with a daughter of my age whom he clearly adored.

Though little Emily was my true love, I was struck by Agnes's air of quiet happiness.

I must have Agnes near me. The thought of ever losing her...

I noticed that evening that Mr. Wickfield drank too much.

I said good night to Mr. Wickfield's clerk, Uriah Heep.

I suppose you are quite a great lawyer.

Oh no, I'm a very umble[2] person.

He was studying to improve his legal knowledge.

Perhaps one day you'll be a partner in Mr. Wickfield's business.

Oh no, Master Copperfield, I am much too umble for that!

He kept twisting and writhing in a snaky sort of way.

What a clammy hand he had – like a fish.

I rubbed mine afterward, to warm it and to rub away his touch.

1. Canterbury: an ancient cathedral city in Kent, in the southeast of England. The archbishop of Canterbury is the head of the Church of England.
2. umble: Uriah Heep's way of saying "humble."

OLD FRIENDS AND NEW PLANS

At 17 I was not sure what I wanted to do in life.

You need to go into the world and look about you. You could start by visiting those friends in Yarmouth.

Whenever I am in trouble or fall in love in earnest, I shall ask your advice.

Why, you have always been in earnest.

I was sad to take leave of Agnes and the dear old house. They had become so much a part of my life.

Trotwood, I feel I can ask no one but you. Have you noticed an alteration in Papa?

I think he does himself no good by a habit of his[1] which has grown worse since I first came.

And when he is most unfit Uriah seems always to have some business to put before him.

It is that that makes him worse. He knows he is muddled then and cannot understand the issues.

At a coaching inn on the way to Yarmouth, a voice from the past made me forget all cares.

Steerforth! You don't remember me, I'm afraid.

My God! It's little Copperfield.

He had no pressing business and thought it would be amusing to come with me to Yarmouth.

Why, that you two gentl'men should come tonight of all nights!

Em'ly, my darling, here's Mas'r Davy's friend, the gentl'man you've heerd on,[2] come to see you.

Emily was to marry Ham, who had always adored her.

Steerforth rejoiced as much as anyone, so his comment to me later was unexpected.

That's rather a chuckle-headed[3] fellow for the girl, isn't he?

I know you're joking. You more than anyone enter into other people's happiness.

I believe you are in earnest! I wish we all were.

1. a habit of his: his drinking (David and Agnes are both too polite to use the actual word).
2. heerd on: heard of.
3. chuckle-headed: silly.

20

David Copperfield

I spent most of my time at Peggotty's house. When we met in the evenings, Steerforth sometimes seemed troubled.

I wish with all my soul I had been better guided. I wish I could guide myself better!

Oh Ham, I am not as good as I ought to be. You should have found someone steadier, not vain and changeable like me.

Poor little tender-heart!

I was surprised a few days later to find Emily in tears and Ham trying to comfort her.

My aunt took me to Doctors' Commons[1] in London. She thought the career of proctor might suit me.

We propose an initiatory month.[2]

It cost my aunt £1,000 to article me[3] to Mr. Spenlow. She rented rooms for me near the Commons. Steerforth suddenly turned up there with two friends and we had a riotous party.

Steerforth — you're the guiding star of my existence.

We went on to the theater. Agnes was in the audience! I had no idea she was in London, and was horrified that she had seen me drunk. Next day she asked me to call.

Ah, Agnes! Always my good angel.

If I were your good angel, Trotwood, I would warn you against your bad angel.

If you mean Steerforth, you wrong him very much.

I do not judge him from what I saw last night, but from many things in your account of him. Something tells me that you have made a dangerous friend.

She told me Uriah Heep was in London on business.

Disagreeable business, I fear. I think he is going to enter into partnership with Papa.

Uriah! That mean, fawning[4] fellow! You must prevent it while there's time.

It is forced on him. Uriah takes advantage of Papa's weaknesses. In a word, Trotwood, he is afraid of him.

1. Doctors' Commons: the headquarters of a society of civil lawyers, known as proctors. They dealt with Church and navy matters, with wills and with marriage settlements.
2. an initiatory month: a month's probationary trial period. 3. to article me: to make me a trainee lawyer. 4. fawning: wheedling and flattering.

21

LOVE AND DISHONOR

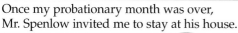

Once my probationary month was over, Mr. Spenlow invited me to stay at his house.

Mr. Copperfield, my daughter, Dora.

I told Papa I *must* come out.

It's the brightest time of the day, don't you think?

Grrr!

I fell headlong in love. I adored everything about Dora Spenlow.

It is very bright to me now, though it was very dark a minute ago.

Do you mean a compliment, or has the weather really changed?

The weather hasn't changed — I meant the state of my feelings.

Later, at a stuffy dinner party, I was delighted to find my old schoolfriend Traddles, now studying to be a barrister.[1]

My lodgings are very modest, but Mr. and Mrs. Micawber are excellent company.

Mr. and Mrs. Micawber! Why, I am intimately acquainted with them!

The Micawbers, Traddles, and I enjoyed a happy and quite sober supper in my rooms. Mr. Micawber's difficulties were the same as ever.

Mr. Micawber must throw down the gauntlet[2] to society. He must advertise.

I quietly advised Traddles not to lend anything to Mr. Micawber. My guests had gone and the fire had burnt low when I heard steps on the stairs.

I have brought you a letter from Yarmouth.

I thought you said you were in Oxford. Have you been there long?

A week or so.

1. barrister: a lawyer who pleads in court.
2. throw down the gauntlet: issue a challenge.

Peggotty's letter said that Barkis was very ill. I decided to visit at once. Steerforth made an odd remark.

Think of me at my best, if we are ever parted.

Barkis was "going out with the tide," as the fishermen say.

Here's Ham to take you home. What, Em'ly? Let you stay with uncle?

She's sorrowful and frightened, like. I'll leave her till morning.

Emily seemed to shrink from Ham and cling to her uncle.

Poor Barkis died that night.

Mas'r Davy, will you come outside a minute?

After the funeral, Ham came back to the boat-house alone.

She's gone! Em'ly's run away!

I pray my good and gracious God to kill her sooner than let her come to ruin and disgrace![1]

What am I to say indoors? How shall I break it to him?

Ham thrust a letter into my hand.

Read it slow, please. I don't know as I can understand.

"When I leave my dear home it will be never to come back."

"Pray heaven to have pity on my uncle. I never loved him half so dear."

"My last tears and my last thanks for Uncle."

Who's the man? For the Lord's love don't tell me his name's Steerforth!

Mas'r Davy, it ain't no fault of yours, but his name's Steerforth and he's a damned villain!

I'm going to seek my niece throughout the wureld.[2]

I'm going to find my poor niece in her shame and bring her back.

1. ruin and disgrace: By 19th-century standards, a woman who runs away with a man is disgraced forever.
2. wureld: Mr. Peggotty's way of saying "world."

My Aunt Brings News

Meanwhile, Dora was always in my thoughts. Once, after a picnic, she asked if the ride had tired my horse.

It was a long way for him, for he had nothing to uphold him on the journey.

Wasn't he fed, poor thing?

I mean he had not the unutterable happiness that I had in being near you.

In a moment, I had Dora in my arms. I said I loved her to distraction, I would die for her. The more I raved,[1] the more Jip barked.

Yip yip yip!

Dora and I were engaged! I told no one but Agnes. I felt it warming my whole being as I returned home one evening – to a great surprise.

Aunt! Mr. Dick! What an unexpected pleasure.

Let me draw up the sofa for you.

It's all I have. My money was invested badly and it's gone.

All I have in the world is in this room, except the cottage, which is let.

Thank you, Trot. I prefer to sit on my property.

This was a blow indeed, and not only for my aunt. Until I qualified as a proctor, I depended on her money.

I was nearing home the next day when a cab drew up and a familiar face looked out.

Agnes! Of all the people in the world there is no one I could wish to see more!

No one?

Well, perhaps Dora first.

Certainly Dora first, I hope.

1. raved: spoke excitedly.

My aunt seemed anxious to explain to Agnes how she had lost her money. She had ignored Mr. Wickfield's advice and re-invested it herself.

Dear Miss Trotwood, is that all the story?

It's enough, child. If there had been more to lose, Betsey would have thrown that after the rest, I don't doubt.

Agnes looked relieved that her father was not to blame. She had another reason for being in London.

Papa is here on business, and that means Uriah Heep is here too.

I do not want my father to come alone with him.

Oh, Trot! There is such a change at home.

Uriah lives with us now he is a partner, and he seems always to come between father and me.

I finally told my aunt about Dora.

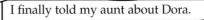

My dear aunt, no one can form the least idea of what she is!

Oh, Trot, Trot, Trot. So you fancy yourself in love. The little thing is very fascinating, I suppose.

Not silly? Not light-headed?

I had never thought to ask myself this. It was a new idea to me.

You expect to go through life like two pretty pieces of confectionery.

She spoke with such a gentle air that I was touched.

We are young and inexperienced, I know, but we love each other truly.

Ah, Trot, blind, blind, blind![1]

---

1. blind, blind, blind: Miss Trotwood refers to the expression "love is blind," meaning that people do foolish things without thinking of anything but their love.

Uriah Spreads His Influence

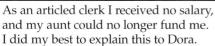

As an articled clerk I received no salary, and my aunt could no longer fund me. I did my best to explain this to Dora.

Oh, don't be dreadful. Don't talk about being poor and working hard!

And Jip must have a mutton chop every day at 12.

My dear, we must be brave and fight our way ahead.

If you could read a cookery book I would send you...

But I realized Dora was almost in fits with panic. I begged her forgiveness and we made up.

Meanwhile, something had finally turned up for Mr. Micawber.

I am contracted to Mr. Uriah Heep to be his confidential clerk.

I have always been of the opinion that Mr. Micawber possesses the judicial mind.[1]

He took his new responsibilities very seriously.

May I take the liberty of suggesting that we draw a line.

On one side of the line is the whole range of the human intellect, with one trifling exception.

On the other is that exception — the affairs of Wickfield and Heep.[2]

I visited Agnes. What a pleasure it was to see her calm face smiling up at me.

When I come to you I come to such a sense of rest. My reliance is on you.

But it must not be on me, Trotwood. It must be on someone else.

On Dora?

Assuredly.

I explained about the cookery book and "fighting our way ahead."

Oh, Trotwood — being so sudden with such a timid, loving, inexperienced girl. Poor Dora!

---

1. the judicial mind: the mind of a lawyer.
2. On one side…On the other: He means that he is happy to talk to David about anything except his work, which is confidential.

Uriah was always hovering near her.

Do you suppose that I regard Miss Wickfield otherwise than as a very dear sister?

Do you keep watch on Miss Wickfield?

All's fair in love, Sir. You're quite a dangerous rival, Master Copperfield.

You may not, you know. But then, you see, you may.

For the sake of Miss Wickfield let me tell you...

...I am engaged to another lady.

And I believe Agnes Wickfield is as far removed from your aspirations[1] as the moon itself.

In the charity school they taught us to be umble to our betters, and really, it ain't done bad!

My Agnes! Would you be so good as to call her Agnes, Master Copperfield?

I know you have never liked me as I have liked you, Master Copperfield.

All along you've thought me too umble, I shouldn't wonder.

What a malicious, revengeful spirit his upbringing had bred!

Uriah encouraged Mr. Wickfield to drink till he was befuddled. But when Uriah hinted at marrying Agnes, Mr. Wickfield rose from the table with a cry.

You will never sacrifice yourself[2] from a mistaken sense of duty, Agnes?

Stop him, Copperfield, or he'll say something he'll be sorry for.

Look at my torturer! Before him I have step by step abandoned name and reputation, peace and quiet, house and home.

You and me know what we know, don't we, Mr. Wickfield?

Dear brother, you have nothing to fear. The step you dread my taking I shall never take.

1. removed from your aspirations: beyond what you can hope to reach.
2. sacrifice yourself: agree to marry Uriah.

THE WANDERER

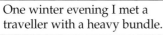

One winter evening I met a traveller with a heavy bundle.

Mas'r Davy! It do my heart good to see you, Sir. Well met, well met.

Mr. Peggotty and I went to a quiet inn.

I'll tell you wheer all I've been and what-all we've heerd. We've heerd little, but I'll tell you.

She used to talk about them coasts with flowers always blooming and the sea dark blue.

I know'd that's where he'd take her.

I've been through France and into Italy — mostly a-foot, sometimes in market carts.

I got news of her being seen among them Swiss mountains.

I made for them mountains day and night. But I was too late and they was gone.

He showed me a fat bundle of banknotes. They were from Steerforth.

I'll go ten thousand mile to lay that money down afore him.

If I do that, and find my Em'ly, I'm content.

And Ham, how is he?

He ain't no care for his life. When there's hard duty to be done, he steps forward afore all his mates. Yet he's as gentle as a child.

As we parted, it seemed as though the snow-wrapped city was hushed in reverence for the solitary figure that went into the night.

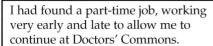

I had found a part-time job, working very early and late to allow me to continue at Doctors' Commons.

How shall we live without, Dora?

Don't do it. Why should you?

How? Anyhow!

Everyone treated Dora as a pretty toy, much as she treated Jip. I tried some playful education.

Would you know how to buy a shoulder of lamb for dinner?

Why, the butcher would know how to sell it, and what need I know, silly boy!

She tried to keep accounts, but the figures only made her cry.

They won't add up!

The cookery book was put in a corner for Jip to stand on. Dora was delighted.

Dora and Agnes became good friends.

If I had always had Agnes for a friend, I might have been much cleverer.

My love — what nonsense!

I have forgotten what relation Agnes is to you.

No blood relation, but we were brought up together like brother and sister.

I wonder why you ever fell in love with me?

Perhaps because I couldn't see you and not love you, Dora.

Suppose you had never seen me at all.

Suppose we had never been born!

29

FOUND!

I turned 21, and Dora and I were married.
Mr. Dick was best man.

Are you happy now, foolish boy, and sure you don't repent?

It was wonderful to come home to Dora each evening. But the half-cooked meals were not so wonderful.

Don't you think it would be better for you to remonstrate with[1] Mary Anne?

I couldn't. I am such a little goose and she knows it.

Dora was terrified of the cook.

All the shopkeepers seemed to cheat us. But Dora did her best. She gave a supper for Traddles.

Oysters, dear.

My love, what have you got in this dish?

What a happy thought!

The tops won't come off!

Dora had not asked the fishmonger to open the oysters. And I did wish that Jip had not been encouraged to walk on the table.

My aunt was fond of Dora and never got cross with her.

Don't you think that you could advise and influence Dora a little?

Trot, no! Don't ask me such a thing!

Remember your mother's second marriage and don't speak of exerting an influence.

Value Dora for the qualities she has and forget those she has not.

This is marriage, Trot; and heaven bless both of you in it, for the pair of babes that you are!

My aunt was right. I loved my wife dearly and was happy, but it was not quite the happiness of my dreams. There was something missing.

30

1. remonstrate with: argue with, criticize. Mary Anne is a typical name for a servant; servants were not always called by their real names.

In the street one day I recognized Steerforth's manservant. I asked where his master was.

Oh, Emily!

He went off and left me to tell her he was gone.

If she had had a knife, she would have killed herself, I think.

I left Mr. Steerforth's service while we were abroad with the young person from Yarmouth.

I locked her up for her own safety, but she got out.

Never heard of since — dead, for all I know.

I told Mr. Peggotty what I had learned.

My niece Em'ly is alive, Sir.

I don't know how 'tis, but I am told as she's alive.

We thought it most likely that Emily would make for England.

She won't go home.

She'd come to London. Where else could she lose herself so readily?

It was a Yarmouth woman, a schoolmate of Emily's, who finally led us to her miserable lodgings.

Uncle!

You have made up your mind as to the future?

Mas'r Davy, I thank my Heavenly Father for having guided of me, in His own ways, to my darling.

We will emigrate together. No one can't reproach my darling in Australia. We will begin a new life!

Mr. Micawber's Finest Hour

A letter from Mr. Micawber:

"My peace is shattered. The canker is in the flower. The cup is bitter to the brim."

He asked Traddles and me to meet him in London.

Gentlemen — I am a straw upon the surface of the deep and am tossed in all directions by the elephants —

— I beg your pardon; I should have said the elements.

I cannot bear it any longer. I shall speak out.

I shall redress[1] the wrongs inflicted by that hypocrite and perjurer[2] HEEP!

We all met at Canterbury. Mr. Micawber led us to Uriah's office and flung open the door.

Miss Trotwood, Mr. David Copperfield, and Mr. Thomas Traddles.

Oho! This is conspiracy!

Miss Wickfield, you had better not join that gang.

I am the agent and friend of Mr. Wickfield, Sir, and I have a power of attorney[3] from him.

The old ass has drunk himself into a state of dotage[4] and it has been got from him by fraud.

Something has been got from him by fraud. We will refer that question to Mr. Micawber.

My charges against — HEEP:

When Mr. Wickfield's business faculties grew weak, HEEP obtained his signature to documents by false pretenses.

1. redress: set right.
2. hypocrite: a dishonest person who pretends to be honest; perjurer: a person who lies while swearing to tell the truth.
3. power of attorney: a legal document which confirms that Traddles is allowed to act on Mr. Wickfield's behalf.
4. dotage: complete helplessness.

32

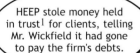

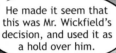

HEEP stole money held in trust[1] for clients, telling Mr. Wickfield it had gone to pay the firm's debts.

HEEP then pretended that he had lent him the money to pay back the stolen funds.

This pocket book contains HEEP's imitations of Mr. Wickfield's signature.

He made it seem that this was Mr. Wickfield's decision, and used it as a hold over him.

The bond[2] was signed Wickfield and Micawber — both forgeries.

In this way he made sure Miss Wickfield would never want her father's affairs looked into.

While I thought your father had made away with it, Agnes, I kept quiet, but I'll have it out of this fellow.

We can now prove, through HEEP's false accounts, that Mr. Wickfield has been deluded and plundered in every conceivable way by the false and grasping HEEP.

Where are the account books?

I want my property!

They are now in the hands of Mr. Traddles.

Threatened with prison, Uriah returned the money. The Micawbers were triumphant.

Australia was the solution! My aunt, in gratitude for regaining her property, offered him the money he needed.

I wonder you have never thought of emigrating.

It was the dream of my youth.

I could not receive it as a gift, but perhaps as a loan —

— allowing time for something to turn up...

I am sure he had never thought of it in his life.

1. held in trust: held for safekeeping.
2. The bond: the legal document recording the imaginary loan from Heep to Mr. Wickfield.

Dora Leaves Us

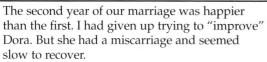

The second year of our marriage was happier than the first. I had given up trying to "improve" Dora. But she had a miscarriage and seemed slow to recover.

When I can run about as I used to do, I shall make Jip race. He is getting slow and lazy.

I suspect it's age, Dora. It's a complaint we're all liable to.

We may keep one another company a little longer!

We thought Dora would soon be running about again. But I carried her upstairs every night and each time she felt lighter in my arms.

Within a few weeks I was no longer carrying her but sitting by her bed.

Will you tell Agnes that I want very much to see her —

— and then I have nothing left to wish for.

Except to get well again, Dora.

I am going to say something that I have often thought lately.

Ah, Doady.[1] Sometimes I think that that will never be.

Doady dear, I am afraid I was too young.

I listened with a stricken heart as she spoke of herself as in the past.

1. Doady: Dora's nickname for David.

I don't mean in years only, but in thoughts and everything.

I have begun to think I was not fit to be a wife.

I was very happy, but as the years went on my boy would have wearied of his child-wife.

Oh Dora, love, as fit as I to be a husband!

It is better as it is.

When you go downstairs, send Agnes to me.

And while I speak to her, let no one come in — not even Aunt.

While Agnes was with Dora, I sat alone with Jip.

Whimper!

Not tonight, Jip!

He gave a plaintive cry and stretched himself at my feet as if to sleep.

But he was not asleep. When I patted him I knew that he would never stir again.

Oh, Agnes! Look, look here.

I turned and saw Agnes's face, so full of pity and grief, and her hand upraised towards heaven.

Agnes?

It was over. Darkness came before my eyes, and for a time everything was blotted from my memory.

TEMPEST

The death of Dora shattered my spirit. But I wanted to see the Peggottys and the Micawbers off to Australia. Mr. Peggotty came to me with a request.

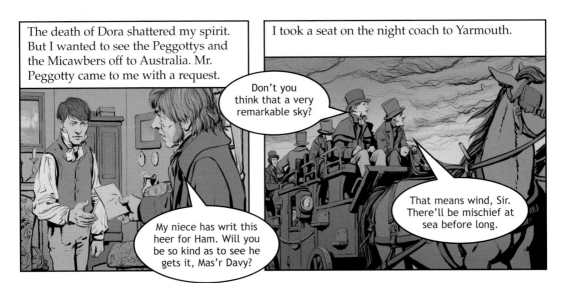

My niece has writ this heer for Ham. Will you be so kind as to see he gets it, Mas'r Davy?

I took a seat on the night coach to Yarmouth.

Don't you think that a very remarkable sky?

That means wind, Sir. There'll be mischief at sea before long.

A furious wind arose. It rained in gusts like showers of steel. We were seriously afraid the coach would be blown over.

At Yarmouth the wind was driving in from the sea, raising gigantic walls of water.

Fishermen's families were gazing anxiously out to sea. There was no sign of Ham.

I was woken at the inn next morning early by a loud knocking on my door.

A wreck close by, Sir. Make haste if you want to see her. She'll go to pieces any minute.

The ship was rolling like a desperate thing. The sea, sweeping over the deck, was carrying men, casks, and planks into the water like toys.

A cry went up as the wreck parted in the middle. The last survivor waved his red cap cheerily. The gesture reminded me vividly of someone I knew.

Lifeboats could do nothing in such waves. A man came forward with a coil of rope. It was Ham. I tried to stop him.

Mas'r Davy, if my time is come, 'tis come. If 'tan't, I'll bide it.[1]

Lord above bless you, and bless all.

He made two attempts to reach the wreck. But a vast hill of water rose and crashed, and Ham and the ship were gone.

They carried his body to the nearest house. I still had Emily's letter in my pocket.

Sir, will you come over yonder?

Has another body come ashore?

Do I know it?

Fragments of the old boat-house, blown down in the night, were scattered over the beach.

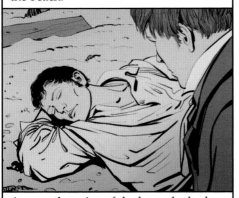

Among the ruins of the home he had wrecked lay Steerforth – with his head resting on his arm, as I had so often seen him lie at school.

I hid the deaths from Mr. Peggotty. He and Emily would bear the truth better when they had made a new home.

This is no separation. It is merely crossing. The distance is quite imaginary.

Peggotty and I went aboard to say farewell. The Micawbers and the Peggottys, now firm friends, were settling in cheerily.

1. If 'tan't, I'll bide it: If it hasn't come, I'll wait for it.

A New Life

I spent three years travelling. When I returned, my aunt and I talked far into the night.

And when, Trot, are you going over to Canterbury?

Agnes had never been out of my thoughts. I had taught her to think of me as a brother, but I understood now, when it was too late, what she really meant to me.

Has Agnes any...

Any what?

Any lover?[1]

She might have married twenty times since you have been gone.

My aunt seemed thoughtful. She gazed at me for some minutes.

I suspect she has an attachment, Trot.

A prosperous one?[2]

I can't say. She has never confided in me.

I rode to Canterbury the next day. Agnes was so good and dear to me, I could not find words for what I felt. I talked of my travels instead.

Now, Agnes, tell me of yourself. If you have a secret, let me share it. Let me be your brother.

Agnes! Sister! Dearest! What have I done?

I am not myself. Don't speak to me now.

I understood, then, something that I had not dared to think of.

I went away, dear Agnes, loving you. I returned home loving you.

I have loved you all my life.

1. Any lover: anyone who wants to marry her.
38   2. A prosperous one: one who is likely to succeed.

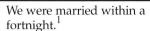

We were married within a fortnight.[1]

Dearest husband, I have one thing more to tell you. That night that Dora died, she made a last request of me —

— that only I should occupy this vacant place.[2]

She wept, and I wept with her, though we were so happy.

Ten years later:

At the close of my story, I see my aunt, some fourscore[3] years and more but upright yet, and good old Peggotty always at her side.

I see Mr. Dick, happy and free.

And Traddles, happily married and sure to become a judge.

Mr. Peggotty, white-haired yet hale and hearty, returned to visit us. It had been a hard struggle at first, he said, but now he was thriving.

And Emily?

Liked by young and old.

She might have married well, but "Uncle," says she, "that's gone forever."

And the Micawbers? Mr. Peggotty handed me a newspaper cutting reporting a public dinner held in honor of the distinguished magistrate,[4] Wilkins Micawber Esquire.

To the ornament of our town. May he never leave it!

My lamp burns low and it is time to close the book.

I have written far into the night, but the dear presence of Agnes bears me company, as I pray it may do when I close my life.

1. a fortnight: a period of fourteen days.
2. occupy this vacant place: replace Dora as David's wife.
3. fourscore: eighty.
4. magistrate: a judge in a local court.

The End

CHARLES DICKENS (1812–1870)

Charles Dickens was easily the most popular novelist writing in English in the 19th century, and many people would agree that he was the greatest.

He was born in 1812 to moderately well-off parents (his father was a naval clerk), but the family's lifestyle changed when his foolishly extravagant father was arrested for debt and sent to the Marshalsea, a notorious debtors' prison. While Charles's mother and the younger children joined his father in the prison, Charles, who was only 12, was sent to live alone in a lodging house in North London. There he worked 12 hours a day in a boot-blacking (shoe polish) factory to earn the family some money. He never forgot this experience. It taught him the conditions in which poor people lived and worked. Later, as a successful novelist, he used his writing to expose such injustices.

An engraved portrait of Charles Dickens

BECOMING A WRITER

The family's fortunes improved enough for Dickens to return briefly to school, but at 15 he had to start work as a clerk in a solicitor's office. He escaped from this boring job by teaching himself shorthand and becoming a parliamentary journalist. He was a quick and lively reporter with a great relish for oddities of character. Soon he was writing humorous articles based on his observations of London life. A collection of these, published in 1836 as *Sketches by Boz*, was such a success that he was immediately invited to write another book. This was *The Pickwick Papers*, which appeared in 1837 and was a runaway success.

SERIALS

From this moment Dickens never looked back. As soon as one book appeared, his readers were impatiently waiting for the next. He was constantly at work, often starting on a new book while he was still writing installments of the previous one. All his major novels first came out as serials in magazines. This meant that people who couldn't afford the price of an expensive three-volume novel could still buy his work. This was important to Dickens, who loved to feel he was in touch with a wide public and could stir their consciences through his writing.

A BUSY LIFE

Dickens had enormous energy. As well as completing 14 full-length novels and countless shorter pieces, he was also a journalist, magazine editor, lecturer, travel writer, playwright and amateur actor. He used his acting skill to great effect in giving public readings from his novels, mesmerizing audiences by his ability to conjure up vivid characters. He took these performances on tour in England and the United States. One particularly gruelling series of 76 readings which he gave in America in the winter of 1867–1868 finally broke his health, and he died two years later, aged 58. He was at work on his unfinished novel *The Mystery of Edwin Drood* on the day before he died.

DICKENS THE SOCIAL CRITIC

In his novels Dickens was a fierce critic of the poverty and inequality he saw all around him in Victorian society. He campaigned for parliamentary reform, better schooling, better housing and sanitation, and for the abolition of slavery. His greatest asset in getting people to think seriously about these things was his ability to entertain. His novels are all good stories, packed with characters whose quirks and oddities can be sinister, endearing, or hilarious, and who all have that larger-than-life quality that we still call "Dickensian."

BOOKS BY CHARLES DICKENS

1836: *Sketches by Boz*
1837: *The Pickwick Papers*
1838: *Oliver Twist*
1839: *Nicholas Nickleby*
1841: *The Old Curiosity Shop*
1841: *Barnaby Rudge*
1843: *A Christmas Carol*
1844: *Martin Chuzzlewit*
1845: *The Cricket on the Hearth*

1850: *David Copperfield*
1853: *Bleak House*
1854: *Hard Times*
1857: *Little Dorrit*
1859: *A Tale of Two Cities*
1861: *Great Expectations*
1865: *Our Mutual Friend*
1870: *The Mystery of Edwin Drood*
 (unfinished)

DICKENS'S FAVORITE WORK

O f all his novels, Dickens loved *David Copperfield* the best. In his preface to the 1867 edition he wrote: "Like many fond parents, I have in my heart of hearts a favorite child. And his name is David Copperfield."
He was thinking of the book itself, not of David as a person. He re-read it before starting work on *Great Expectations* (he wanted to make sure he didn't repeat himself, as both stories are told in a similar way by their main character), and was shaken by the strong effect it had on him. He confessed to his close friend John Forster that this was because he had put so much of his own life into it. Like David in the book, Dickens had a happy childhood at first, and, like David, he found this security suddenly snatched away.

A CRUEL CHILDHOOD

Dickens was 12 when his parents tried to boost their income by sending him to the boot-blacking factory; David's experiences are much worse. An orphan child abused by a cruel stepfather, he is only 10 when the Murdstones turn him out into the world. When he runs away from the factory, he has to walk more than 60 miles (95 km) from London to Dover, selling his clothes to get a crust to eat, in order to reach his only living relative.

None of this happened to Dickens. But the need to describe a suffering childhood comes directly from his early experience – his sense of betrayal by his parents. He could not get over their lack of concern for him. It left a scar that never healed. He was a boy with a sense of his own worth, doing well at school, loving books, expecting to study for a career. It seemed to him that his parents did not care that all his chances were being thrown away.

His bitterness at being denied an education is clearly echoed in the novel. When David leaves school for his mother's funeral, the Murdstones do not bother to send him back:

And now I fell into a state of neglect, which I cannot look back upon without compassion…. What would I have given, to have been sent to the hardest school that ever was kept! – to have been taught something, anyhow, anywhere! No such hope dawned upon me.

Even bitterer are the words Dickens puts into David's mouth when he speaks of his loneliness as a working child in London:

…it is a matter of some surprise to me, even now, that I can have been so easily thrown away at such an age. A child of excellent abilities, and with strong powers of observation, quick, eager, delicate, and soon hurt bodily or mentally, it seems wonderful to me that nobody should have made any sign in my behalf.

The 12-year-old Dickens thought he faced a lifetime in the factory. It was to be little more than a year. After a brief return to school (under a brutal headmaster who was the model for Mr. Creakle) he was out in the world again, fending for himself at the age of 15.

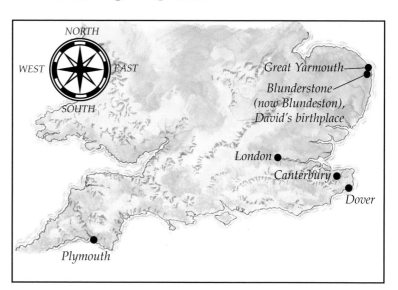

SUCCESS AT LAST

David's early career is clearly based on Dickens's own. Like David, Dickens worked for a law firm, became a reporter, and then found his true calling as an author. Like David, he fell hopelessly in love when very young. In the long run, Dickens's life was a success story, and so is David's. In the novel's closing pages he is surrounded by a loving wife and children, he has wealth and fame, and everyone dear to him has found some form of happiness.

SPEAKING UP FOR OTHERS

With some of the quirkiest characters that Dickens created, *David Copperfield* is on the whole an upbeat novel. But there is a thread of pain running through it. Dickens wants his readers to understand the harm that uncaring people do to the powerless – in Mr. Murdstone's treatment not only of David but of his mother; in Miss Murdstone's relentless dislike of him; in Mr. Creakle's cruelty to the boys in his care; in the unthinking way David is sent out, unprotected, into the world.

This was the sort of cruelty that many well-off families inflicted on their children through a belief in stern discipline. But when Dickens describes David's life at the bottling factory he is speaking on behalf of the vast numbers of poor children who were neglected and exploited in Victorian England. The amount of factory work they could be expected to do had recently been limited by law to 10 hours a day! (Yet still those in work were the lucky ones. It is estimated that there were up to 30,000 children living rough on the streets in mid-Victorian London, "filthy, roaming and lawless.") Dickens the campaigner is reminding his readers that it is the unfeelingness of those in power that allows the exploitation of the powerless to continue.

PLACES IN THE STORY

Area shown on main map

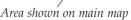

Dickens is famous for his ability to create striking and memorable characters. Some of them have become so famous that their names are known even by people who have never read a Dickens novel.

THE HEROINES

David Copperfield has two heroines. The reader realizes, long before David does, that he is destined for wise, patient Agnes, but it is Dora who comes to life more vividly in the novel. Dickens pulls off the difficult job of convincing us that a person who would have been such a pain in real life is actually intensely lovable. It helps that shrewd Aunt Betsey thinks the world of her, but, more than anything, it is the depth of David's feeling for her that makes Dora's charm believable and her death genuinely sad.

The feeling rings true because it is Dickens's own. He had fallen headlong in love at the age of 18 with a banker's daughter called Maria Beadnell. She was small, slight, and very pretty, with adorable ringlets. This is Dora exactly, and although Dickens does not record that love smote him like a bolt from the blue the instant he set eyes on her (as happens to David), it is easy to believe that it did. He worshipped Maria for four years, though she had many admirers and would not commit herself. "I have never loved and can never love any human creature breathing but yourself," he wrote, in a final appeal to her. She did not reply, but at the time of writing *Copperfield* he was still treasuring her memory.

There is an unromantic sequel to this story. Twenty-two years after their parting, the world-famous author suddenly received a letter from Maria, now Mrs Winter and with two grown daughters. They began writing to each other; Dickens's emotional letters show that he thought of her as quite unchanged. He asks if she has read *David Copperfield* and recognized in it "a faithful reflection of the passion I had for you…and in little bits of Dora touches of your old self." They arranged a meeting, which was a disastrous mistake. "Dora" had become a very stout middle-aged matron, and boring too. Dickens was writing *Little Dorrit* at the time. He makes its hero meet his once-enchanting love of 25 years ago and find her fat, over-talkative, and silly. Poor Maria! Did she recognize herself? To one of his readers who had enjoyed this character – who is named Flora Finching – Dickens wrote: "We have all had our Floras. Mine is living, and extremely fat."

THE ECCENTRICS

The novel has some of Dickens's greatest comic creations. Best known is Mr. Micawber, partly based on Dickens's father. You'd think that a character who owed money everywhere and was always coaxing loans from friends would be dislikable. Far from it. He is one of the most lovable people in the book, kindly, warm-hearted, never intending to defraud a soul. An incurable optimist (except in his suicidal moments), he means to pay off every debt "when something turns up."

Unluckily, that moment is always just around the corner.

Short of money but never short of words, Mr. Micawber is famous for delivering what must be runner-up as the most famous piece of advice in English literature:

"Annual income twenty pounds, annual expenditure nineteen nineteen six, result happiness. Annual income twenty pounds, annual expenditure twenty pounds ought and six, result misery."[1]

It is second only to Polonius's "This above all – to thine own self be true…" (Shakespeare, *Hamlet*, act I, scene 3). Not so high-minded as Polonius's, but as harsh truth, founded on the speaker's experience, it is second to none.

It's difficult to believe that anyone as shrewd as Uriah Heep would have given Mr. Micawber a job, but we have to accept it for the plot's sake. It is good to know that in Australia his luck changed and Mrs. Micawber's touching faith in him ("Mr. Micawber will be – a page of History") was finally justified.

David's eccentric great-aunt, Miss Betsey Trotwood, is another great creation. She's first met through the window, like the wicked fairy not invited to the christening, and goes off in a huff for the oddest reason. But later she proves to be David's fairy godmother in disguise. She is mannish and cranky and doesn't care what anyone thinks of her, but her off-putting manner hides a heart of gold. She is full of common sense, a good judge of character, and a loyal friend. Dickens also gives her unusual powers of sympathy and understanding. Much

in advance of her time, she believes that mental illness can be helped by kindness, and takes into her home the likable Mr. Dick, whose relatives had put him in an asylum. Her views are Dickens's views, of course.

THE VILLAIN

What becomes of that slippery weasel Uriah Heep? He tries to swindle the Bank of England and ends up behind bars. David meets him during a tour of an expensive new prison whose inmates are all in solitary confinement. Heep is as slimy as ever, blessing the system for showing him the error of his ways and recommending it for everyone. He completely fools the governors, who see him as living proof that shutting people up does them a world of good. Dickens is making the point that prisons solve nothing. To reduce crime, the money would be better spent on schools or housing for the poor.

1. For an explanation of shillings and pence, see page 10 note 2. "Nineteen nineteen six" means £19, 19s, 6d (19 pounds, 19 shillings, and sixpence), which is 6d less than £20; "twenty pounds ought and six" is £20, 0s, 6d (20 pounds, no shillings, and sixpence), which is 6d more than £20.

Answer to Mr. Murdstone's question on page 10: £93, 15s, 0d (93 pounds, 15 shillings, no pence).

When *David Copperfield* appeared in 1850, there was already a flourishing industry in stage adaptations of Dickens. Around 240 productions had been derived from his earlier novels, *Nicholas Nickleby* and *Oliver Twist* being the most popular. Due to the feeble copyright laws of the time, theater managers were free to get stage versions written cheaply and rushed into production even while the novel itself was still being serialized. Dickens regarded this piracy with mingled pleasure and fury. It was excellent publicity for a new book, but it distorted the plot and took liberties with his characters – and he earned nothing from it.

In the case of *Copperfield*, the first off the mark was veteran "pirate" George Almar. His *Born with a Caul, or the Personal Adventures of David Copperfield* opened at the Strand theater in London in October 1850, before the last installments of the novel had appeared. Two other stage versions were up and running in New York by the end of that year.

Nineteenth-century versions liked to focus on the aspect of *David Copperfield* that modern readers find hardest to accept – the fate of little Emily, saved from endless shame by her uncle's love. Theater managers knew that melodrama always went down well, and Emily's story had all the right ingredients: anguish, heroic death, and redemption through a life of self-denial. The most popular version was Andrew Halliday's four-act *Little Em'ly*, which opened almost simultaneously on both sides of the Atlantic in 1869. By the end of the century it had gone through no fewer than 24 different productions.

DICKENS THE PERFORMER

Apparently Dickens approved of Halliday's version, but by this time he was joining in the business of Dickens stagings himself, with his hugely popular public readings. Selections from *Copperfield* were a regular part of the program. Audiences were overwhelmed by his rendering of the storm scene and the tragic death of Ham Peggotty.

Originally these readings had been charity performances, but it soon became plain that this was a way for the novels to make extra money for their author instead of someone else. In his later years Dickens found lengthy reading tours more profitable than writing; but in the end they exhausted him and probably contributed to his death.

THE SILVER SCREEN

A huge surge in *Copperfield* plays followed Dickens's death. Forty-eight separate adaptations appeared in the 1870s alone. The novel remained a favorite for staging, right up to the time when a new form of public entertainment took over.

David Copperfield was one of the first novels to be told on screen, in an American silent film of 1911. At that date reels of film only came in short lengths, so the story had to be split into three episodes – *The Early Life of David Copperfield*, *Little Em'ly and David Copperfield*, and *The Loves of David Copperfield* – which were released separately over a period of three weeks.

One of the very first full-length films was an English *David Copperfield* of

1913. In 1922 there was a Danish version. Since the coming of the talkies there has been a steady stream of *Copperfields*, in the cinema and on TV. A hugely successful Hollywood version from 1935 is remembered for its kindly, heart-warming Micawber played by W. C. Fields, a famous American comedian who normally produced a stereotype of himself – hard-bitten and cynical – in every role he took. Which just shows that Mr. Micawber brings out the best in everyone!

The 1970 centennial of Dickens's death was marked by a film that rallied all the great names in postwar English theater: Laurence Olivier (Mr. Creakle), Michael Redgrave (Daniel Peggotty), Ralph Richardson (Mr. Micawber), and Edith Evans (Aunt Betsey). Unfortunately the star-studded cast was let down by an uninspiring screenplay.

SERIALS

Television serialization, which allows a story to develop in installments over a period of time, is ideally suited to Dickens, who organized his novels in a similar way. A 13-part *David Copperfield* appeared on TV in 1956, and versions have cropped up regularly since. A 1999 TV film has Daniel Radcliffe (of Harry Potter fame) as the young David and Maggie Smith as

Emily on the beach at Yarmouth: an illustration by 'Phiz' (Hablot Knight Browne) for the 1850 edition.

Aunt Betsey. An American/Irish version in 2000 has an additional storyline for the Murdstones. In 2009 the Italians made a version for their TV.

NOW FOR SOMETHING DIFFERENT

There have been animated *David Copperfields*: an Australian one in 1982 and an American version in 1993, in which the characters are animals (David is a cat). But the award for worst adaptation goes perhaps to the 1981 Broadway musical *Copperfield*. It closed after 13 nights – "A clunky, often incoherently told melodrama," according to *The New York Times* theater critic, that "manages to miss the human comedy, the tears, and even the point of Dickens's novel . . . it's hard to imagine what parent – short of an evil Dickensian one – would take the family to [it]."

IF YOU ENJOYED THIS BOOK, YOU MIGHT LIKE TO TRY THESE
OTHER TITLES IN BARRON'S *GRAPHIC CLASSICS* SERIES:

Adventures of Huckleberry Finn Mark Twain

Beowulf Anonymous

Dr. Jekyll and Mr. Hyde Robert Louis Stevenson

Frankenstein Mary Shelley

Great Expectations Charles Dickens

Gulliver's Travels Jonathan Swift

Hamlet William Shakespeare

The Hunchback of Notre Dame Victor Hugo

Jane Eyre Charlotte Brontë

Journey to the Center of the Earth Jules Verne

Julius Caesar William Shakespeare

The Last of the Mohicans James Fenimore Cooper

Macbeth William Shakespeare

The Merchant of Venice William Shakespeare

A Midsummer Night's Dream William Shakespeare

Moby Dick Herman Melville

The Odyssey Homer

Oliver Twist Charles Dickens

Robinson Crusoe Daniel Defoe

Romeo and Juliet William Shakespeare

A Tale of Two Cities Charles Dickens

The Three Musketeers Alexandre Dumas

Treasure Island Robert Louis Stevenson

20,000 Leagues Under the Sea Jules Verne

White Fang Jack London

Wuthering Heights Emily Brontë